KIDS' SPORTS STORIES

SKATEBOARDING PALS

by Elliott Smith

illustrated by Amanda Erb

PICTURE WINDOW BOOKS

a capstone imprint

Published by Picture Window Books,
an imprint of Capstone
1710 Roe Crest Drive
North Mankato, Minnesota 56003
capstonepub.com

Library of Congress Cataloging-in-Publication Data
Names: Smith, Elliott, 1976- author. | Erb, Amanda, illustrator.
Title: Skateboarding pals / by Elliott Smith ; [illustrated by Amanda Erb].
Description: North Mankato, Minnesota : Picture Window Books, [2022] |
Series: Kids' sports stories | Audience: Ages 5-7. | Audience: Grades K-1. |
Summary: Greta and her new friend Pilar team up to prove
that girls can skateboard just as well as boys.
Identifiers: LCCN 2021004167 (print) | LCCN 2021004168 (ebook) |
ISBN 9781663909541 (hardcover) | ISBN 9781663921345 (paperback) |
ISBN 9781663909510 (ebook pdf)
Subjects: CYAC: Skateboarding—Fiction. | Friendship—Fiction.
Classification: LCC PZ7.1.S626 Sk 2022 (print) | LCC PZ7.1.S626 (ebook) |
DDC [E]—dc23
LC record available at https://lccn.loc.gov/2021004167
LC ebook record available at https://lccn.loc.gov/2021004168

Designer: Tracy Davies

33614082394478

Printed and bound in the USA. 4270

TABLE OF CONTENTS

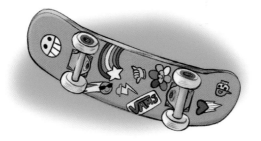

GLOSSARY

 **goofy-foot**—skating with your right foot at the front of the board and pushing with your left foot

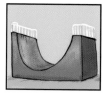 **half-pipe**—a U-shaped ramp with high sides used by skateboarders

 **ollie**—a maneuver where the skater kicks the tail of the board down while jumping to make the board pop into the air

 **shred**—to skateboard with great ability

 **skate park**—an area with ramps and other structures for skateboarding

Chapter 1
AT THE SKATE PARK

Greta ran outside with her birthday present. A skateboard! She put on her pads and helmet. Then she slowly got on the board. She was rolling!

Greta had always wanted to try skateboarding. She had watched other kids at the nearby **skate park**, and it looked fun. Now, she was doing it!

Her mother watched as Greta skated
slowly up and down the street.

"This is so much fun!" Greta shouted.

After she skated around the block a few times, Greta was ready for a new challenge.

"Mom, can I go to the skate park?" she asked.

"Yes, but I'm coming with you," her mom said. "You've just started learning."

"No problem," Greta said confidently.

Greta and her mom walked to the skate park. There were lots of kids there. She saw a few from her school. Some were doing cool jumps off ramps. Others were skating down into a big bowl and coming back up.

Instead of starting slowly, Greta walked
over to the bowl and put her board down.
She saw that her mom was talking to
another parent. Now was her chance for
a big trick!

"What are you doing here?" a voice
said. It was a boy in her class named
Bryce. "Girls can't skate."

"Yes, we can!" Greta said angrily. With that she hopped on her board and went down into the bowl. But Greta didn't realize how fast she would go.

CRASH! She landed flat on her stomach. Her board rocketed away.

Bryce skated down and started laughing. "I told you," he said with a smirk.

Another boy skated down too. "Cut it out," the boy said to Bryce. He held out his hand to Greta. "My name is Luke. Are you okay?"

"Yes," Greta said, holding back tears.

Greta grabbed her board and walked over to her mom.

"Can we go home now?" Greta asked softly as she looked down.

"Sure. Did something happen?"

"I will tell you when we get home," said Greta.

Chapter 2
A NEW FRIEND

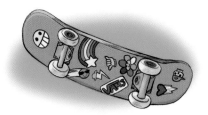

After coming home from the skate park, Greta put her board in the closet. Mom came in and sat on the bed.

"So what happened?" she asked.

Greta told her the story about the skate park and Bryce. "I don't think I want to skate anymore," she said.

"Well, I don't think you should quit
because of one fall," Mom said. "And I
think there's someone you should meet."
Mom told her they had new neighbors
with a girl about Greta's age.

"Cool!" Greta said. She went outside to introduce herself.

As Greta walked down the street, she saw a girl coming toward her holding a skateboard.

"Hi, my name is Pilar," she said. The bottom of her board was covered with colorful stickers.

"You like to skate?" Greta asked.

"Yeah, I love it," Pilar said. "My dad built me a ramp for practice."

Greta was thrilled to have a new friend who was also a skater.

"Can we skate together?" Greta asked excitedly. Pilar nodded. Greta ran home and got her board.

Pilar and Greta spent the next few weeks skating. Pilar was good. She even rode **goofy-foot**! Pilar showed Greta some simple moves to help her stay balanced.

Before long, Greta could do some small tricks like flipping her board with her feet.

The girls started using Pilar's ramp. Pilar could soar off the ramp and land cleanly. Greta was a little more cautious. Still, she was having fun with her new friend.

"Maybe we should check out the skate park," Pilar said one day.

Greta gulped. "Sure," she said quietly.

Chapter 3
SECOND CHANCE

Greta was nervous as they walked to the skate park. She was thinking about Bryce. And about falling. She told Pilar what had happened the last time she went to the park.

"Hey, don't worry," Pilar said. "We'll have fun. And I've got your back."

The park was filled with skaters. Just as she feared, Greta saw Bryce skating toward them.

"Back for more falls?" Bryce said. "I told you, girls can't skate."

Pilar stepped forward. "Girls can do anything," she said. "Let's go **shred**, Greta."

Greta and Pilar skated toward the big bowl. "You can do this," Pilar said. "Just like we practiced. We'll go together."

Greta was afraid. But she took a deep breath. She thought, *I can do this.*

Pilar went first. Greta followed. *ZOOM!*
Greta balanced herself on the board. She
shot up the other side without falling!

"Yes!" Greta shouted as she stopped. She
fist-bumped Pilar.

They skated over to the **half-pipe**.
Bryce was waiting for his turn. He went
down the half-pipe but lost his balance
coming back up. He skidded on his knee
pads.

"Nice try," Greta said.

Pilar went next. Her move on the
half-pipe was perfect!

"Okay, Greta, it's your turn," Pilar said. "Try to do an **ollie**."

Greta was ready. She approached the ramp and crouched down on the board. She went down and flew up in the air on the other side. She turned in midair and aimed for a landing spot. She kept her balance. She landed it perfectly!

"Awesome move!" Bryce said. "Uh, I'm sorry about before. Maybe we can all skate together?" Bryce looked at them hopefully.

Greta looked at Pilar and smiled. "Sure," she said. "But you'll need to keep up with us!"

MAKE YOUR OWN STICKERS

Do you want to decorate your helmet, skateboard, or other sports gear like Pilar? Try making these cool stickers.

What You'll Need:
- tape
- contact paper
- markers
- scissors

What You Do:
1. Tape down the contact paper, shiny side up, on a table.
2. Draw whatever designs you would like on the paper with markers. Make them colorful!
3. Cut out your designs and peel off the backing of the contact paper. Stick it on your skateboard and other gear!

REPLAY IT

Take another look at this illustration. How do you think Greta felt when Bryce laughed at her? How would you feel?

Pretend you are Greta. Write a note to Pilar thanking her for being such a good friend and helping you get your confidence back.

ABOUT THE AUTHOR

Elliott Smith is a former sports reporter who covered athletes in all sports from high school to the pros. He is one of the authors of Capstone's Natural Thrills series about extreme outdoor sports. In his spare time, he likes playing sports with his two children, going to the movies, and adding to his collection of Pittsburgh Steelers memorabilia.

ABOUT THE ILLUSTRATOR

Amanda Erb is an illustrator from Maryland currently living in the Boston, Massachusetts, area. She earned a fine arts degree in illustration from Ringling College of Art and Design. In her free time, she enjoys playing soccer, learning Spanish, and discovering new stories to read.